A Squash and a Squeeze

Spot the Difference Book

Based on the bestselling picture book by

Julia Donaldson and Axel Scheffler

MACMILLAN CHILDREN'S BOOKS

Tiny House

Find and circle eight differences between the pictures of the little old lady.

Tick the boxes as you find them.

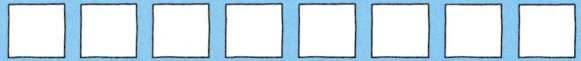

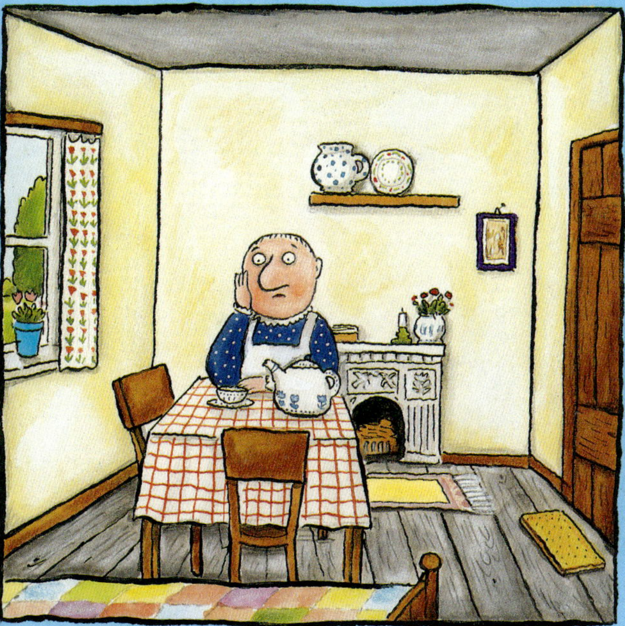

Odd One Out

Circle the wise old man that is different from the rest.

Help Me, Please!

The little old lady asks the wise old man for help.
Find and circle eight differences between the pictures.

Fireplace Finds

The hen broke a jug.
Circle five differences between the pictures.

Feeding Time

Find and circle eight differences between the pictures of the larder.

Little Old Lady

Circle the little old lady that is different from the rest.

Fiddle-De-Dee

The little old lady is glad to have the house to herself.
Find and circle eight differences between the pictures.

Farmyard Fun

Find the row of farm animals that is different from the rest.